The Surprise Visit

Danielle Star

Scholastic Inc.

Published by Scholastic Inc., *Publishers since 1920*,
557 Broadway, New York, NY 10012. SCHOLASTIC and associated logos
are trademarks and/or registered trademarks of Scholastic Inc.

ISBN 978-1-338-28176-7

Text by Danielle Star
Original title *Il giorno della felicitá*
Original Italian language edition published by RCS Libri S.p.A. (Fabbri Editoir)

Editorial cooperation by Carolina Capria and Mariella Martucci
Illustrations by Erika De Pieri, Nicoletta Baldari, Barbara Bargiggia, Emilio Urbano, and Patrizia Zangrilli
Graphics by Danielle Stern

Special thanks to Tiffany Colón
Translated by Chris Turner
Interior design by Baily Crawford

10 9 8 7 6 5 4 3 2 1 18 19 20 21 22

Printed in the U.S.A. 40
First printing 2018

Contents

Imagine a magical land wrapped in golden light. A planet in a distant galaxy beyond the known stars. This enchanted place is known as Aura, and it is very special. For Aura is home to the pegasus, a winged horse with a colorful mane and coat.

The pegasuses of Aura come from four ancient island realms that lie within Aura's enchanted oceans: the Winter Realm of Amethyst Island, the Spring Realm of Emerald Island, the Day Realm of Ruby Island, and the Night Realm of Sapphire Island.

A selected number from each realm are born with a symbol on their wings and a hidden magical power. These are the Melowies.

When their magic beckons them in a dream, all Melowies leave their island homes to answer the call. They must attend school at the Castle of Destiny, a legendary castle hidden in a sea of clouds, where they will learn all about their hidden powers. Destiny is a place where friendships are born, where Melowies find their courage, and where they discover the true magic inside themselves!

Map of Aura
The Spring Realm
The Winter Realm

The Day Realm
Castle of Destiny
The Night Realm

Map of the Castle of Destiny

1 Butterfly Tower—first-year dormitory
2 Dragonfly Tower—second-year dormitory
3 Swallow Tower—third-year dormitory
4 Eagle Tower—fourth-year dormitory
5 Principal Gia's office
6 Library
7 Classrooms
8 The Winter Tower
9 The Spring Tower
10 The Day Tower
11 The Night Tower
12 Waterfall
13 Runway
14 Assembly hall
15 Garden
16 Sports fields
17 Cafeteria
18 Kitchen
19 Auditorium

1
2
5
3
6
7
8
4
9
12
10
11
13
15
14
16
17
18
19

Meet the Melowies

Cleo

Her realm: unknown
Her personality: impulsive and loyal
Her passion: writing
Her gift: something mysterious . . .

Electra

Her realm: Day
Her personality: boisterous and bubbly
Her passion: fashion
Her gift: the Power of Light

Maya

Her realm: Spring

Her personality: shy and sweet

Her passion: cooking

Her gift: the Power of Heat

Cora

Her realm: Winter

Her personality: proud and sincere

Her passion: ice-skating

Her gift: the Power of Cold

Selena

Her realm: Night

Her personality: deep and sensitive

Her passion: music

Her gift: the Power of Darkness

1
A Warm Welcome

"Eggs, butter, flour, vanilla . . . ," Maya repeated, going over and over the ingredients she needed for the cupcakes she wanted to bake. She was trotting down the big staircase in the Castle of Destiny, the school for Melowies.

Maya loved cooking more than anything, and being allowed inside the huge kitchen in the castle would be very exciting. Students weren't normally allowed in there, but this was a special occasion. So that morning, Maya had jumped out of bed before the others were awake to ask Theodora, the school cook, for permission to bake cupcakes in the kitchen.

When she got to the kitchen door and heard a rattle of pots and pans on the other side, Maya was still going over the recipe: "Blend the butter and sugar, add the eggs . . ." She knocked, poked her head through the door, and smiled a big smile. "Good morning, Theodora! Do-you-think-I-could-use-the-kitchen-to-bake-some-cupcakes-please?"

Busy with a pie, the pegasus with the

cocoa-colored mane looked at her with a puzzled expression.

"I didn't quite catch that, sweetheart, but good morning to you, too!" Theodora smiled.

"Sorry, I'm a little nervous!" chuckled Maya. "Let me explain. My mom was a student at the Castle of Destiny a long time ago. Principal Gia has asked her to come back and talk to the students about her career as a healer. I know the kitchen is your place, but my mom is coming today, and I would really love to be able to make her something special!"

"I think that's a wonderful idea, dear!" exclaimed Theodora, squeezing Maya into a vanilla-scented hug. "What type of cupcakes were you thinking of making?"

"I was thinking of making her favorite," Maya

said. She showed Theodora the recipe in her notebook. "I have a few—"

"Oh, sweetie, no. We do not use recipes in this kitchen. We let our noses be the guide."

"B-b-but . . . ," Maya stammered. "I don't think I know how to do that."

"Well, my dear, you are about to learn," Theodora said, handing her a bowl.

Maya loved to cook and bake, but making cupcakes without a recipe to follow was impossible!

"Umm . . . do you think I should add more sugar?" she asked after she had blended a few ingredients together.

"Don't ask me! Ask the batter!" Theodora answered.

Maya stared into the bowl. It was easy

enough to ask the question—any question, really—but she was pretty sure the batter wasn't going to talk back to her. At least not in a way she could understand.

"What is it telling you?" Theodora asked.

"More sugar!" Maya announced, feeling very pleased with herself. She added a spoonful of sugar and stirred it in. Then she added a little more of this and a little bit of that, smelling and tasting as she went. Soon she thought the mixture was ready to go into the oven.

"Wow, something smells

great!" cried Electra, who had just walked into the kitchen with Cora, Selena, and Cleo.

"What are you guys doing here?" Maya asked, surprised to see her roommates. Theodora ran over to hug Cleo, the Melowy she had raised after Principal Gia found her on the steps of the school.

"We have been looking everywhere for you, Maya," Cleo said, escaping from Theodora's sweet hugs. "You have to come with us now! Everything is ready for your mom's arrival!"

"You go on ahead," said Theodora, peeking into the oven. "I can finish up here."

"Thank you so much! Let's go!" Maya smiled. "I'm so ready to see her."

"You are going to change, right?" Cora asked, looking Maya up and down. "This year's fashion doesn't really include the floured-and-chocolate-coated look."

Maya looked at her reflection in a baking tray to see that her mane was all covered in flour and there was chocolate on her face. She blushed. "Well, I'm *almost* ready!"

For days, the students at the castle had been buzzing about the famous healer from the Spring Realm coming to speak to them. The fourth years, whom she would be addressing, were going to welcome her with a choreographed dance. All the students were assembled in the garden, waiting to watch the performance.

"They are all so good," Electra said while performing some rather silly dance steps. "And just think—one day we will be just like them."

"You guys will be. Not me. Look at Flora—I will never be that good," Maya said, pointing to one of the most talented fourth-year students. Flora was a Melowy from the Spring Realm whose red hair was tied back in braids. She was practicing flying in graceful circles in the clouds.

"Of course you will!" cried Cora. "All it takes is practice and commitment."

"Actually, you will be even better because you will be more . . . *you* than she is." Cleo smiled.

"Girls, our guest is here!" called Principal Gia. "Please take your places."

The Melowies all lined up just as a shape appeared in the sky. "Is that her?" Selena asked.

Maya nodded happily, recognizing her mother's graceful flying style.

"Oh, she is very beautiful!" said Cora. "Do you think she could teach me to do my hair like that?" As the figure grew closer, they could see someone was behind her. Maya felt a thrill spread through her wings. She couldn't quite make out who it was, but she sure hoped it was her brother!

2
The Surprise

"Leo!" Maya exclaimed, flying to hug her brother.

"Maya!" cried the little pegasus with the orange mane.

"He wouldn't let me leave without him!" said Amaryllis. "I hope it's okay with Principal Gia. He has missed you so much. Are you happy to see us?"

"I am so happy!" Maya cried, giving

her mom a big hug. "I have missed you both, too. I don't think Principal Gia will mind."

"Welcome back to the Castle of Destiny," announced Principal Gia, trotting over to them. "It must be strange to be back! And welcome to you as well, Leo. We are so honored to have you as our guest. The students will be so lucky to hear you speak about your experience."

The principal caught Flora's eye and signaled them to begin their performance. The filly confidently led her classmates to the middle of the garden.

"To thank you for coming today, the students have prepared a short performance," said Gia, flapping her wings gently.

With that movement, the leaves of the trees began to rustle, making a sound almost like a melody. Flora took off, followed by her classmates. Hovering in the sky and moving as one, the Melowies performed a dance routine that left the audience breathless.

Maya was so overwhelmed that she didn't know where to look: at the dance, at her mother, or at her brother. This was definitely going to be a wonderful day.

* * *

"Quick, quick!" called Electra, turning back to look at her friends as they rushed to their geography class. "We are so late!"

After the ceremony, the five Melowies had stayed behind with Amaryllis and Leo to bring them the cupcakes Maya had made, and they had lost track of time.

"There you are at last!" said Ms. Pangea, looking up from the roll with a stern expression when they walked into the classroom. "Come along, now. Go and sit down. We were all waiting for you." The five friends didn't need to be told twice and walked quickly to their seats.

"Something tells me that Ms. Pangea is going to be asking a lot of questions today," Selena whispered, taking her place near her roommates and staring up at the animated maps of the four realms of Aura that hung on the walls. "My head is pounding, and that's what always happens right before she asks a lot of questions."

"Let's hope you are wrong." Maya sighed, wrapping her wings tightly around herself.

"No, she's right," Cora agreed. "She is wearing her emerald necklace, and whenever she wears that necklace, she always asks a ton of questions. Accessories never lie!"

"But we studied together yesterday. You should know everything!" Electra said.

Maya shrugged. "Yes, but I was a little distracted about my mom coming, and I was too excited to really concentrate."

"Maya!" Ms. Pangea called suddenly. "Could you sum up for the class what you read last night?"

"I . . . I . . ." Maya hesitated as she tried to think of some excuse not to answer the question.

"If Maya doesn't know the answer, I would be happy to tell you," said Eris, a pushy Melowy who never missed a chance to show off to the teachers. She was always trying to make Maya and her friends look bad.

"No, no!" Cleo said. "Maya can answer. Can't you, Maya? Just give her a moment to think." Cleo turned to Maya and gave her a look that could make Maya confident enough to do anything, no matter what. Even get up on a runway in old pajamas in front of the whole school.

"I guess so," Maya whispered. She stood

up and went to the front of the class. She surprised herself by giving a perfect summary of the chapter they had read the night before. Her friends were impressed, but Eris was cranky as ever.

3
Baby Games

The sun shone more brightly than ever on the Castle of Destiny that afternoon. Almost all the students were enjoying the beautiful day.

Eris, though, was trotting nervously between the shelves in the library. Ms. Circe, the librarian, noticed that she was in a bad mood. This was the perfect opportunity! A while ago, the Supreme Ruler had asked her to find a student who could be a sort of

spy and pass along secret information about what went on in the castle. Ms. Circe was sure Eris was the perfect Melowy for the job.

"Hello, Eris," she said. "Is something wrong?"

"This morning in geography, Maya answered every question and got the top grade in the class," Eris complained. "I would have done much better than her, but I didn't even get the chance!"

"Of course you would have. You are the best student in the whole school," Ms. Circe said, sure that her words would have the desired effect.

Eris's eyes grew wide. "Do you really think so?"

"Absolutely! I have even decided to give you an important job. I want you to keep an eye on the other Melowies and let me know if they do anything strange."

Eris looked puzzled. "Why?" she asked.

Ms. Circe could not tell her the truth: that she was hoping to get information that would help the Supreme Ruler carry out her evil plan. She had no choice but to lie. "Principal Gia wants to get to know the students better. I will pass the information on to her. It is very important that we keep this a secret. You must talk to no one else about it, just me."

"You can count on me," Eris said, eyes sparkling.

Eris left the library feeling very proud of herself. Ms. Circe thought she was the best student in the school and trusted her enough to give her a special job!

* * *

Later that day, Eris was out in the garden spying for anything interesting she could pass on to the librarian. She saw Maya and Leo playing ball. *Now is my chance to get even with that know-it-all*, she thought.

"Looks like you two are having fun," she said to them.

"Oh, hi, Eris!" Maya answered happily. "Yes, we haven't seen each other in a long time and—"

"Look out!" Leo shouted.

Maya smiled, easily catching the ball and throwing it back to her brother. She turned to Eris. "We are playing this game that—"

"It looks like a game for losers," Eris cut her off.

Maya looked at her in disbelief. She wanted to tell Eris off, but she got so nervous and couldn't think of what to say.

"You might be good at answering teachers' questions, but seeing how much fun you are having out here playing with your baby brother shows me you're just a loser."

“Hi, girls!” said Flora as she came walking past. “Some of us are going to Sugar and Spice for a milk shake. Would you like to come?”

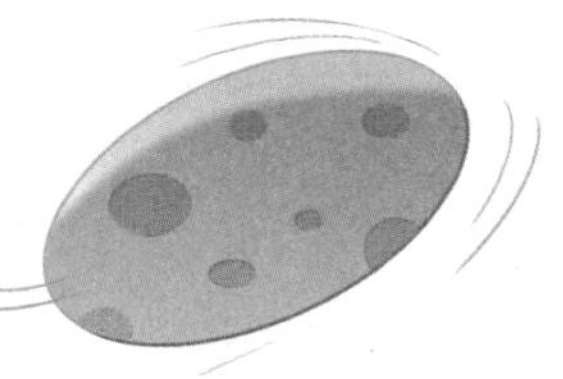

“Absolutely I would!” Eris immediately answered, feeling flattered by the invitation from a fourth-year student. “But I bet Maya won’t. She’s too busy playing with her little brother.”

Maya nodded as she blushed. She never thought there was anything wrong with having fun with Leo, even if he did like games that were for younger kids. The things Eris said and the way Flora looked at her made her feel so uncomfortable.

"Look out!" Leo yelled, and before Maya realized what was going on, the ball hit her right in the head.

"I'm so sorry, Maya!" Leo cried, feeling terrible.

"Are you okay?" Flora asked.

"No," Maya answered, completely embarrassed. She walked away and pretended to look for the ball in the bushes, trying to put as much space between herself and the giggling behind her as possible. She felt as if everyone in the garden was laughing at her. She was so embarrassed!

4
A Picnic with Friends

"Does it hurt?" Cora asked. She put a bag full of ice that she had conjured up using her powers on Maya's head.

"No," Maya said, staring down at her bedspread.

"Are you sure you're all right?" Cleo asked, sharing a questioning look with her roommates.

I don't think she is, Electra answered with her eyes.

Not at all, Selena agreed with hers.

Maya forced herself to smile and jumped out of bed. "Of course I am all right!" she said. "It was just a silly accident. I'm going to study for a little while."

"It's Wednesday. We don't have Art of Powers class today," Cleo said. "Since you started your afternoon by getting hit in the head with a ball, I think we should just do something fun for the rest of the day."

"We could go get something to eat at Sugar and

Spice," Selena suggested. "I'm sure Leo would love one of Zoe's milk shakes."

"I don't think so. If Leo fills up on sweets, he'll be bouncing off the walls and get a stomachache. Mom will get annoyed with me," Maya objected.

"We could have a picnic in the Neon Forest!" Electra suggested. "Today in geography class, I zoomed in on the map and studied it really closely. We've seen only one small part of it, but there is a lot more. There are meadows full of beautiful flowers, which would be perfect for a picnic!"

"That sounds great! We should go ask Principal Gia right away," Cleo said, heading for the door. The five Melowies rushed out of Butterfly Tower and down the passageway that led to the main tower of the castle, then climbed the great spiral staircase until they arrived at the principal's office, on the top floor.

They knocked on the door. "May we come in?" Cora asked, peeking into the room. She saw Amaryllis and Leo standing near Principal Gia's desk. "Oh, good afternoon!" she said.

"Principal Gia," Selena began. "We were wondering if we could have your permission to have a picnic in the Neon Forest this afternoon."

"That is a lovely idea!" Principal Gia smiled. "You remember the Neon Forest, of course! It's a wonderful place," she said to Amaryllis. "It's just a short fly from here."

Then, turning back to the girls, she said, "But you will have to be careful not to go wandering off into the thickest part of the forest. That area is particularly wild and dangerous."

"We will be sure to stay away from it," Cora said.

The principal nodded. "Then you have my permission. As long as it's okay with your mother, Maya."

Amaryllis nodded.

"Cool!" Leo cried. "Can I come?"

"No," Maya said quickly. "It's not a trip for little kids."

"Pleeeaaseee?" Leo insisted. "I'll be good. I promise."

"Maya, I am sure Leo will be on his best behavior," Amaryllis said.

"B-b-but . . . ," Maya stammered.

"That's okay with us, Maya. We will help you look after him!" said Electra.

"All right." Maya sighed. She reluctantly went along with her friends and her brother as they trotted down the sun-flooded staircase. *Maybe this is just what I need to make me feel better after those Melowies made fun of me*, she thought. *This day might still turn out wonderful.* Her optimism didn't last very long.

On their way out of the castle, they bumped into Eris and her two best friends, who were coming back from Sugar and Spice with Flora. Flora stared at Maya

and Leo as they walked by, while Eris and her friends giggled. Maya blushed once again.

"Maya," Leo asked, "why is it called the Neon Forest?"

"I don't know," she lied, feeling very annoyed.

Electra, Cleo, Selena, and Cora all looked at her. "She doesn't know?!" Electra whispered. "We just learned that in geography. See, something is definitely wrong with her."

"She's hiding something!" Cleo added.

5
The Neon Forest

"Are we there yet?" asked Leo.

"Not yet," snapped Maya.

The five Melowies and the little pegasus had left the Castle of Destiny far behind as they flew toward the Neon Forest, but their destination still wasn't on the horizon.

"Are we there yet?" Leo asked again just a moment later.

Cleo chuckled. "Trust me, Leo, when we get there, you'll know it!"

Just then, a gust of wind blew away a thick blanket of clouds in front of them. Finally, they could see the tops of the enormous trees that grew in the Neon Forest. Maya, Cora, Selena, Electra, and Cleo all smiled. They had learned about it in class, but seeing it with their own eyes was different. Leo stared in wonder.

It was called the Neon Forest because everything that grew there changed bright, brilliant colors as the sun moved across the sky during the day: yellow at dawn, orange at sunset, and then blue in the evening. Each color was so different from the next.

"Now we're here!" exclaimed Leo happily, shooting through the air.

"Hey, where are you going? Slow down!

Don't run ahead!" Maya shouted, struggling to keep up with her brother.

"Yay! Let's go!" Cleo cried a moment later.

The friends let the breeze carry them gently downward, until they landed on a trail just as the whole forest was turning pink around them.

"We should go this way," Electra suggested, studying the map she'd brought with her.

"But look how cool it looks that way!" protested Leo, pointing to a part of the forest where the trees were so thick you could barely see the sky. "Look at all those colors. That's where I'm going!" Then, without waiting for an answer, Leo trotted off.

"Get back here!" cried Maya.

"Come on, it looks like fun!" insisted Leo.

"Principal Gia told us not to go that way. Besides, you have to do what I say, because I'm older and I know what's best for you!" Maya shouted in a bossy voice.

"But I . . . ," said Leo.

"I knew you shouldn't have come!" blurted out Maya. "You're always hanging around, but I'm older and don't want to spend all my time with a little baby doing things that babies do!" Before her brother could answer, Maya strode off along the path that Electra had pointed out. Her roommates followed her, and Leo followed them.

Maya had really hurt Leo's feelings when she yelled at him. But Electra, Cora, Cleo, and Selena could also see that it hurt Maya as well. She hadn't said a single word since she shouted at him, and her eyes were sad. Cora flew over to Maya. "You know," she said, "we all make mistakes. All you need to do is apologize, and everything can go back to the way it was before."

"I didn't mean to be rude to Leo!" Maya whispered. Her eyes filled with tears.

"I'm sure he knows that," said Cleo, who

had just flown over to them, followed by Selena and Electra. Maya stopped.

"But just in case he doesn't, you should tell him right away!" Electra said.

"You're right." Maya nodded.

When Maya turned around to explain herself to Leo, she got a big shock.

6
A Big Scare

"Where's Leo?!" Maya asked, looking around.

"Don't panic, he can't be too far. He was here just a second ago," said Cleo. "Maybe he's fallen behind."

Maya turned pale. "Or maybe he was so upset over how I treated him that he ran off!"

Electra, Cora, Selena, and Cleo gathered close to Maya, trying to calm her down.

"Don't worry!" Selena said. "We'll find him!"

"Of course we'll find him! He's probably just exploring this beautiful forest. Let's start looking right away," Cora urged, trotting back down the trail.

Maya, Selena, and Cora followed the trail, poking their muzzles into every nook and cranny in the forest. Electra and Cleo flew over the treetops, scanning the area from above. Leo seemed to have disappeared.

"We haven't found anything. What about you?" Cora asked Electra and Cleo when they landed.

"Nothing." Cleo sighed.

They were back at the point of the trail where Maya had lost her temper with Leo.

The light was starting to change from pink and orange to light blue, approaching the dark blue of the Neon Forest at night. Maya felt a lump in her throat, and she couldn't hold back her tears.

"It's all my fault. I am a bad big sister!" she cried.

"Don't say that!" Selena said. "You are a great big sister. You rock! Even the best big sisters are not perfect all the time."

"I shouldn't have listened to Eris." Maya sighed.

"Eris?" Selena frowned, confused.

Maya took a deep breath and decided to tell everyone

what had happened in the garden, including the mean things Eris had said, the look Flora had given her, and all the giggling she had heard behind her back.

She told them how upset she'd been and

how she'd taken it out on her own little brother, whom she loved and had always gotten along with really well. She told them about the fun they always had playing tag in the backyard at home and about the time she taught him how to make cookies, and he'd ended up covered with flour from head to toe. And she told them about how much she enjoyed reading him a bedtime story until he'd drop off to sleep.

"Why didn't you tell us this sooner?" Cora asked.

"What Eris said is all nonsense!" Electra added. "Having fun spending time with your brother doesn't make you a baby or a loser. It means you are a good big sister. Eris is just being mean."

"You and Leo haven't seen each other in a long time," Selena added. "It's normal that you two would actually enjoy spending time playing together."

"Eris just wanted to make you feel bad," said Cleo. "Maybe she doesn't understand

how important family is. Plus, she was probably jealous that you answered all those questions right in class. Eris seemed pretty annoyed that we wouldn't let her answer the questions for you."

"That is all true, but Eris isn't important right now," Cora said. "We have to find Leo. That's all that matters."

"You are right." Maya wiped her tears. She pointed to a trail that led off to the left. "Maybe he went that way.

That's where he wanted to go right before I said all those mean things."

The Melowies followed Maya's suggestion and started down the path to the left. They stayed close together as the forest of trees got thicker. It took only a few minutes to realize they had done the right thing.

"Did you hear that?" Maya asked.

They stopped to listen and heard a small voice in the distance.

"That's him!" exclaimed Cleo with a flap of her wings. "Over there, quick!"

7
The Sands of Time

"Leo, we can hear you! Keep talking!" Maya said as loud as she could.

"I'm over here!"

"It's coming from over there," Electra said, diving into the forest, which was now almost a dark blue.

The voice sounded very close now. The girls moved as quickly as they could until they finally saw Leo in the distance. When he saw them, he flew straight toward them. "Maya!

There you are!" cried the little pegasus. But when Leo took another step toward his sister, he began to sink into the ground, which suddenly turned orange all around him.

"What's happening?" Selena shouted.

"I can't move! I'm stuck!" Leo yelled.

"Wait! I'll help you!" Cleo said. She moved closer to him.

"No! Stop!" cried Maya, suddenly remembering something Ms. Pangea had said in class a few weeks ago. "These are the Sands of Time! It's quicksand!"

"Quicksand?!" Leo shrieked in horror as the sand changed from orange to almost black.

Maya flew into the air and grabbed her brother good and hard around his chest. "Don't worry! I'll pull you out of there! I promise," she said.

"Okay." Leo nodded. He was very scared but trusted his big sister. He always had.

"Hey, look. The quicksand is getting lighter," said Electra.

"You're right!" agreed Selena. "It was almost black before."

"Wait, we learned about this in class," Cora said. "The sand changes color depending on how the pegasus touching it is feeling."

"Right, and the more calm you are, the easier it is to get out!" added Cleo.

"Really?" asked Leo hopefully. The quicksand started to turn green, and Leo was able to move just a little bit.

"Hey, you know what I was thinking about today?" Maya said, realizing that she was the only one who could help her brother now. "That time when we were camping and I was so sure I'd seen a monster, but . . ."

"It was just a tree!" Leo laughed, and the quicksand started to turn warmer colors.

Feeling the quicksand loosen its grip on her brother, Maya pulled even harder. "As soon as we get back to the castle, we'll play another game of ball in the garden, okay?"

"Just the two of us?" asked Leo. "That would be cool!" Suddenly, the Sands of Time turned into a spring of crystal clear water, and Maya was able to pull Leo completely out.

"You're free!" Maya cried, setting Leo down on dry land.

"I was so scared . . . ," whispered Leo, giving in to his sister's cuddles. "I'm sorry I ran away and got myself into such a mess. I just wanted to go back to the castle so you could be alone with your friends. Do you forgive me?"

"No," Maya said firmly. Then she smiled. "But only because you're the one who has to forgive me!"

8
Hugs All Around

"We would be honored to have you back any time you want to come visit us again," Principal Gia said, hugging Amaryllis.

"Can I come back, too?" Leo asked.

"Of course you can, darling! You are always welcome here at the Castle of Destiny." The principal smiled.

It was time for Amaryllis and Leo to return to the Spring Realm. All the students were there to see them off.

"I miss you already," Maya said, hugging her mom.

"Me, too, but I know you are in good hands here." She smiled at Cora, Selena, Electra, and Cleo.

"Next time I come, we will play the entire time I am here, okay?" Leo said.

“That’s a promise.” Maya smiled. “I love you.”

“I love you, too. Group hug!” Leo shouted.

“Wow, it’s so nice how close you are,” Flora said, coming out of the crowd.

“Ummm, thanks,” Maya said, confused.

“I think you saw me staring at you both yesterday, and I just wanted to apologize. I hope you didn’t think I was being rude. I have a little brother at home. Seeing you two playing yesterday just made me miss him more.”

Maya was so happy that she had misunderstood Flora.

"Anyway, I'm late for class," Flora said as she rushed off toward the castle.

Eris was waiting for Ms. Circe in the library. They had agreed to meet there every day after school. She would fill the librarian in on everything she'd seen during the day and the gossip that filled the school's halls. Eris was very proud of her mission—soon the principal would know that she was the best student in the Castle of Destiny.

"I took notes so I wouldn't forget anything," she said.

"Did a lot happen?" Ms. Circe smiled when she saw the pages full of notes Eris brought with her.

"I didn't know what would be useful, so I just wrote everything down," Eris said, and she began to read a list of everything that had happened that day. "This morning in literature, the teacher asked Kate a question that she didn't really know the answer to. Leda went to the bathroom three times during geography class. They served pizza for lunch."

"Okay, thank you." Ms. Circe nodded, pushing her glasses up her nose. Perhaps this wasn't such a great idea after all.

"Then I followed a second-year student who took a book out of the library without speaking with you first," she continued. "I passed the principal and Theodora whispering, and—"

"Wait a minute," Ms. Circe interrupted. "What were they saying?"

"Well, I didn't understand a lot, but Theodora was asking Principal Gia if she thought something or other would still be safe inside the castle. That's all I heard, because I followed the student down the hall."

Eris kept talking, but Ms. Circe had stopped listening. She'd already heard what she needed to hear.

"Are you sure?" The voice sounded hollow in the darkest room of the Night Realm.

Ms. Circe nodded. "I think the White Diamond is hidden somewhere in the Castle of Destiny."

"Good work," said the Supreme Ruler.

"If the diamond really is in the castle," came a grim voice as the candlelight flickered, "all we'll need to do is find it and then—"

"And then we'll bring down all of Aura!" another voice interrupted.

The Supreme Ruler eyed the three pegasuses with her. "Our task is more difficult than ever, but never before has our goal been so clear."

Read on for a sneak peek of the next exciting moment in the Melowies' journey:
The Secret Book

The Legend of the Scorpion

The sun was shining brightly just beyond the clouds that surround the Castle of Destiny like an ocean of whipped cream. The rays shone through the castle windows, and a gentle breeze filled the garden. Everything seemed to glow on that special day. Everything except Cleo's mood.

The Harmony Festival was going to start in just a few hours, and she was not interested in joining her friends Selena, Maya, Cora, and Electra. She might have felt a little better if Theodora was there to cheer her up, but the school cook was busy preparing thousands of delicious goodies for the festival.

Cleo decided the next best thing was a book. Sometimes a really good book can cheer you up almost as well as a good friend. Cleo climbed the steps to the library with its gleaming windows and walls covered with books.

"I would like to borrow a book, please," she said as she walked into the library. Suddenly, she realized Ms. Circe, the librarian, was nowhere to be found. Snobby Eris stood behind the desk, smiling.

Just then she heard a voice. "Which book?" Eris said.

"Eris! What are you doing here?" Cleo asked.

EXPLORE DESTINY WITH THE MELOWIES AS THEY DISCOVER THEIR MAGICAL POWERS!

Hidden somewhere beyond the highest clouds is the Castle of Destiny, a school for very special students. They're the Melowies, young pegasuses born with a symbol on their wings and a hidden magical power. And the time destined for them to meet has now arrived.